ALSO BY ANTHONY DELAUNEY

Dash and Nikki and The Jellybean Game
(Book 1 in the Owning the Dash Kids' Book series)

Lilly and May Learn Why Mom and Dad Work
(Book 2 in the Owning the Dash Kids' Book series)

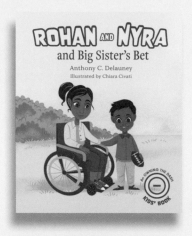

Rohan and Nyra and Big Sister's Bet
(Book 3 in the Owning the Dash Kids' Book series)

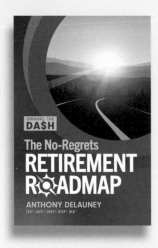

Owning the Dash: The No-Regrets Retirement Roadmap

Owning the Dash: Applying the Mindset of a Fitness Master to the Art of Family Financial Planning

To my daughter, Abbie. Thank you for allowing me to see the world through your eyes. Your kind heart and open mind have helped me understand that good can be found in almost any situation, no matter how chaotic it may seem at the time. You just have to look for it.

MASCOT
KIDS!
an imprint of Amplify Publishing Group

www.amplifypublishinggroup.com

Michael and Hannah and the Magic Money Tree

For more information, please contact:
Mascot Kids, an imprint of Amplify Publishing Group
620 Herndon Parkway, Suite 320
Herndon, VA 20170
info@mascotbooks.com

Library of Congress Control Number: 2023930436

CPSIA Code: PRKF0323A
ISBN-13: 978-1-63755-657-3

Printed in China

MICHAEL AND HANNAH
and the Magic Money Tree

Anthony C. Delauney

Illustrated by Chiara Civati

It was the start of spring break. Such a wonderful day!
The neighborhood children were all ready to go play.
And for siblings Michael and Hannah, their plans were set
for a night of excitement they would never forget.

The Spring Fair had arrived with games, prizes, yummy food,
delicious smells that put everyone in a good mood,
plus fun contests and shows sure to dazzle and amaze
each eager child's senses in the most marvelous ways.

For Michael, Hannah, and their friends, the focus was clear.
A new amusement awaited at the fair this year.
It was something all the children could not wait to see:
a magical and mystical money-making tree.

They had heard terrific tales of the joys it would bring.
With the money tree they could buy almost anything,
like cotton candy, lollipops, and cookies galore,
toys and tiny trinkets, teddy bears, and so much more.

The neighborhood kids had come up with a perfect plan.
They'd be the first to arrive with their tickets in hand.
For there was one firm rule that each child had to obey—
only *eight* kids were allowed to see the tree per day.

So together they all squeezed into a minivan
and buckled up their seat belts before the trip began.
Then off they drove with a line of cars trailing behind.
No one could stay silent. They had so much on their minds.

The van parked at the entrance. The children waved goodbye.
Then they ran to the tallest tent with tickets held high.
They rushed up to a guard standing alone at the gate.
Michael asked, "Did we make it? Please say we're not too late!"

The guard walked into the tent without saying a word. The children stood outside, speechless, until someone heard what sounded like small drums beating behind the tent wall. Suddenly, out sprung a man standing seven feet tall!

"**W**elcome children," he roared out. "You are about to see the majestic, magnificent money-making tree!"
He pulled back the tent flap and signaled them to go through.
"Find a partner," he said, so they entered two-by-two.

Inside it was dark, almost impossible to see,
but lit up at the center stood the giant green tree.
The children sat in a circle and stared at the leaves.
Each had been folded in half. They looked like tiny sleeves.
And inside each leaf, peeking out
  ever so slightly,
dollar bills could be seen,
  tucked inside neat
  and tightly.

Some of the boys were tempted. They reached for the money.
The tall man glared at them with a look not so funny.
He beckoned for the boys to once again take their seats.
He pointed behind them. "Do any of you like treats?"

As the children turned their heads, torches lit up the room. They saw people standing near the walls, each in costume, and in front of all the people were tables with signs that had dollar amounts on them: threes, sixes, and nines.

As they examined the tables, the children could spot
fantastic foods, tempting toys, and candy. A whole lot!
"We are about to begin," said the seven-foot man.
Michael sat up in his chair and quickly raised his hand.
"May I go first?" he begged, shaking his arm in the air.
"One moment," said the man. "There are some rules I must share."

"Together, you and your friends have a choice you can make.
This tree is full of money that everyone can take,
and inside this tent, you can buy all that you can bear.
The game ends when there's nothing left to buy anywhere.

But if before the last purchase, all of you agree
to give everything you bought back and all your money,
you will have another option: to earn your own cash.
Just work the jobs listed here and build up your own stash.
You can earn money for yourself or to help a friend.
What you decide to do, we will find out in the end."

Some children rolled their eyes. *Why work when money was free?*
They all got prepared to go plunder the money tree.
"Ready. Set. Go!" yelled the man, his voice in a hurry.
The kids jumped up and made for the tree in a scurry.

Soon they each had their hands bursting full of dollar bills.
Then they ran to the tables, overcome by the thrills,
and started buying everything their fingers could hold.
It was not long before almost all the things were sold.

As Michael got ready to buy the last of the toys,
he looked around and noticed the other girls and boys.
Some had grins stretching wide with their arms overflowing,
but the others had no hint of any smile showing.

In fact, he saw tears streaming from several friends' eyes.
Their hands were nearly empty, much to Michael's surprise.
All they had was their cash, but with nothing left to buy.
Michael didn't understand what had happened or why.

Hannah cried, "It isn't fair! They were waiting their turn.
It appears for some of us waiting is no concern."
The friends all discussed. *Was there a way to split the loot?*
They squabbled and fussed, hoping to settle the dispute.

Each had a strong opinion on what they thought was fair,
but none of their arguments seemed to lead anywhere.
Hannah whispered to Michael, "Our friends look so upset!"
Michael smiled and said, "We haven't bought the last toy yet."

"We can start over," he said, "and earn cash with each task."
They looked to their friends, and before he could even ask,
the friends cheered. "We agree! The jobs are the fairest way.
This money tree makes it just impossible to play."

The children returned their items.
  Then each picked a chore.
Some selected only one. Others
  chose several more.
A full hour passed before all of the
  jobs were done.
The kids didn't notice. They were
  having too much fun!

In the end, each friend found some things that they could enjoy.
A smile sprung up on the face of every girl and boy.
They bought toys for themselves and treats for one another.
Someone even got a special gift for his brother.

That night, they left the tent knowing better than ever
that free money from a tree is not all that clever,
and that work is a great way to help make money fair
for everyone who wishes to earn his or her share.

ABOUT THE AUTHOR

Anthony Delauney is a financial advisor based in Raleigh, North Carolina, who has a passion for helping families. He is the founder of Owning the Dash, LLC, an organization dedicated to helping educate and inspire families as they work to achieve their financial goals. His other books include *Owning the Dash: Applying the Mindset of a Fitness Master to the Art of Family Financial Planning*, *Owning the Dash: The No-Regrets Retirement Roadmap*, *Dash and Nikki and The Jellybean Game*, *Lilly and May Learn Why Mom and Dad Work*, and *Rohan and Nyra and Big Sister's Bet*.

Michael and Hannah and the Magic Money Tree is Anthony's fourth book in the Owning the Dash Kids' Book series. Anthony wrote this book to entertain children of all ages and to teach them an important financial lesson that will help guide them in the years to come. Many more fun adventures await all the children in the Owning the Dash Kids' Book series!

Special thanks to the Tang family for your support over the years and for your help in bringing the Owning the Dash mission to life in such a fun and engaging way!